D1384378

High overhead, as white as the snow, the first swans were arriving. Each year they come to shelter among the rushes where the sea creeps ashore in long fingers of blue.

And behind them came the north wind, colder than even Grandmother could ever remember. It froze the fingers of water from blue to white, and the swans struggled to find food.

'The swan mustn't die!' declared Kazuo. 'How would the Snow Country Prince feel? We mustn't let him down.'

The people in the village were amazed to see how tenderly the children cared for that poor, sick bird. 'You never give up, do you?' said the old man next-door, and smiled. In fact wherever the children went, it seemed that people's faces broke into a smile . . .

Until the letter came that made their mother cry.

Mama pinned the postcards over Papa's bed. Just seeing them made him feel better. The more cards there were, the better he felt. Stronger and fitter and happier . . . just like the swan!

Even the weather got better day by day. The fingers of sea unfroze, turning from white to blue. The swans sheltering there began to fly away to their spring feeding-grounds. The children carried the injured swan and gently placed it in the water. It lifted its head hopefully towards the sky and flapped its wings.

'Yes, you can do it too! You *can*!' cried Mariko encouragingly. 'Keep trying! Don't give up!'

'No, whatever happens, *don't give up*!' said Kazuo. The words seemed to have been waiting in his heart.

And the wind seemed to sigh the selfsame thing.

One evening, the sky overhead seemed full of swans. Each as white as snow, each as beautiful as the Snow Country Prince himself, they hurtled one by one into the sky until only a single shining swan remained.

'You can do it! You can go too!' called Mariko and Kazuo to the swan they had nursed.

With its feathers dipped in the gold of the setting sun and with a gust of wind beneath its wings, their friend rose into the air to follow the rest.

Then suddenly the tears came. 'First Papa . . . then Mama . . . and now even our swan has gone away!' said Mariko. 'Oh, how lonely winter is!'

But winter was over.
Warmth came back to the Snow Country.
And so did Mama.
And so did Papa – as well and as strong and as happy as any soaring swan on the wing.
So too did the Snow Country Prince, though the children mistook his spring robes for blossom and his words for the soft spring wind when he whispered, 'Well done, Mariko, my Snow Princess! Well done, Kazuo, my Princeling of the Snow Country!'

Oxford University Press, Walton Street, Oxford OX2 6DP
Oxford is a trade mark of Oxford University Press

First translated from the Japanese by Burton Watson

British Library Cataloguing in Publication Data
Ikeda, Daisaku, *1928–*
The snow country prince.
I. Title
895.635 [J]
ISBN 0-19-279886-3

Typeset by Tradepools Ltd., Frome, Somerset
Printed in Hong Kong

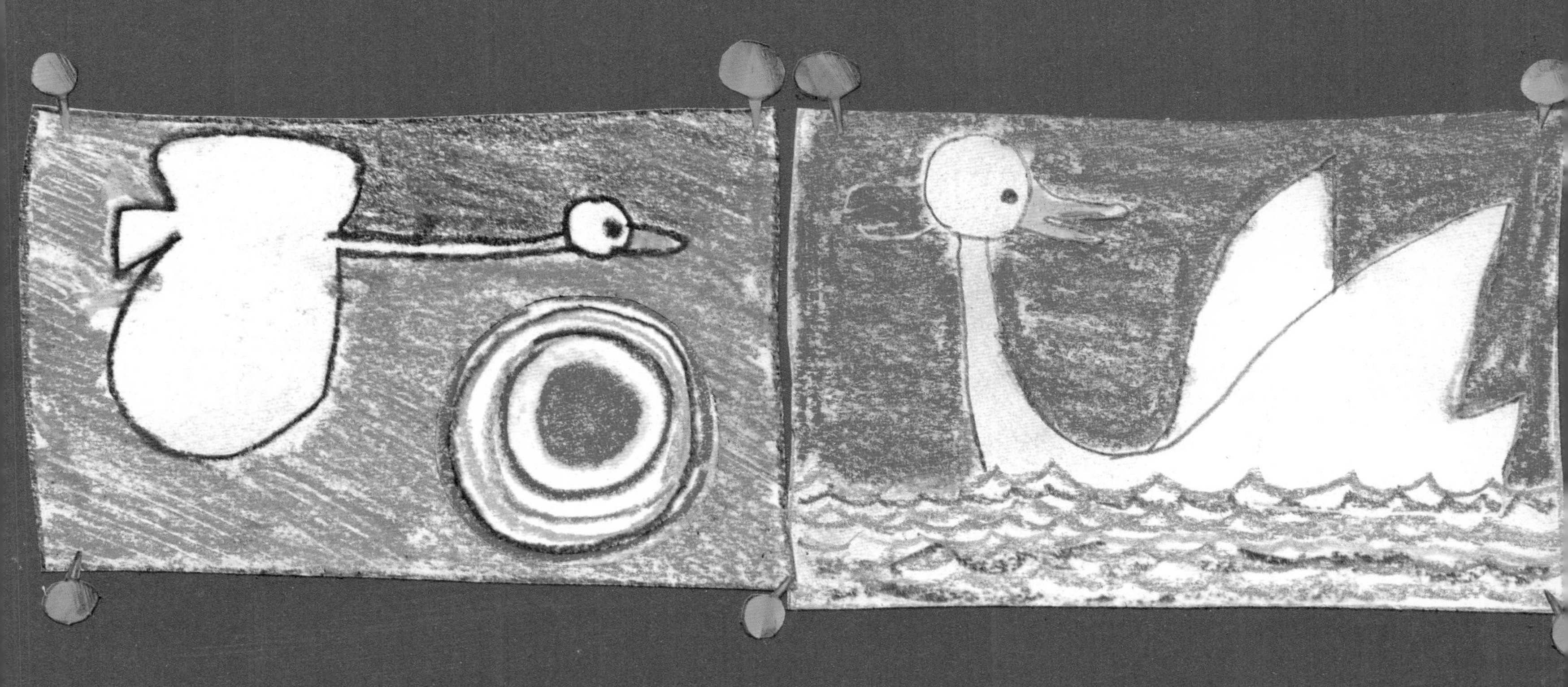